What Is a Friend?

What is a friend?

A friend is someone
who will play with you.

A friend is someone
who will walk with you.

A friend is someone
who will talk with you.

A friend is someone
who will smile with you.

A friend is someone
who will laugh with you.

Who is your friend?